"CANDLES OF ABUNDANT LIGHT"

Let's do your life's work.

Live in the light.

A path to self-reflection, inspiration, growth, & pursued life of light in today's world.

by
Dr. Crystal Davison

Candles of Abundant Light

Let's Live in the Light

Religion-Christian
Inspirational
Self-Transformation
Spiritual
Relationships

Candles of Abundant Light

Copyright © 2019 by Crystal Davison

Davison Publishing - Cypress, Texas

www.crystaldavison.com

Printed in the United States of America

ISBN 978-0-9761150-2-1

Dedication:

I dedicate this book to my husband who challenged me to pay more attention to life on earth, grow in my own way, and shared his candles of light with me to glow more luminously in the light every day.

Thank you and I love you.

Candles of Abundant Light

Mission Statement:

This book is intended to assist in growing and living a life in the light of self with full integrity.

In times of darkness, may you know your given power and shine the light that is *already manifested within you*.

Matthew 5:14-16

Let's Live in the Light

Book Contents:

Life Work Oath:

I want to be a part of the light of the world, which radiates and overcomes the darkness of the days into eternity.

Genesis 1:3-4
Psalm 40:2
Psalm 73:25-26

I am a human.

Genesis 2:7
Job 33:4
Psalm 39:4
Genesis 27:2
Genesis 1:26-27

I am that I am.

Psalm 27:1
Psalm 37:4
1 John 3:1
Romans 5:5

I am light.

John 1:5
Matthew 11:28-30
Isaiah 60:1

Darkness can never overpower the light of
this world.

Thessalonians 4:5
John 1:5
Psalm 34:4
Luke 6:27
Roman 8:35

Let's Live in the Light

I bring light into every space I enter in the world.

Matthew 5:43-48
1 Corinthians 13
Matthew 5:14
John 9:5

I will shine from within and throughout the world.

Deuteronomy 31:6
Isaiah 43:2
Isaiah 60:1
Matthew 5:16

I am strong.

Romans 8:31
2 Corinthians 12:9
John 1:5
Psalm 27:1
Mark 11:22-24

I do not break. I will not fold.

Ephesians 6:10-17
Psalms 4:4
Proverbs 10:25

I am more than enough.

Psalms 23:1
Colossians 3:12
Philippians 4:13
2 Corinthians 9:8

I am love.

1 John 4:8
1Corinthians 14:1
1 Corinthians 13:4-13
Proverbs 10:12
Matthew 5:8

Let's Live in the Light

I live and shine within the agape love.

2 Thessalonians 3:5
1 John 4:16-18
John 15:4
Proverbs 27:19

I am continuously ready to grow and shine brighter.

Galatians 5:22
Psalms 4:6
Psalms 18:28
Ephesians 5:14

Let's Live in the Light

Every new day lived of life experiences
gives us light.

Ephesians 5:8-9
Psalms 118:24
Exodus 15:2

I value my life.

Psalms 139:13-16
Deuteronomy 29:15
Genesis 1:27
Matthew 10:31

Let's Live in the Light

I add value to others' lives.

Proverbs 27:4
1 Thessalonians 5:10-11
Proverbs 10:21 & 32

Timing is ordained and I cannot control events as they happen in my life, which are ordered by a higher power.

Deuteronomy 29:29
Philippians 4:13
Lamentations 3:22-23
Psalms 27:13-14

Let's Live in the Light

I am a part of history.

Psalms 78:4
Deuteronomy 6:5-7
Ephesians 1:4-5
Romans 8:28

Moments of today will compose my life. I define the footprint I leave in the history of time.

James 4:14
Luke 10:20
Philippians 4:6
James 1:7
Proverbs 27:1

Today is part of my eternity.

1 Timothy 6:12
John 3:16
1 John 5:11
2 Corinthians 4:7
Psalms 139:23-24

I understand it's not about
where I am from, but where I am going.

John 14:19-21
Isaiah 41:10
Romans 8:2

Life is not a race, it's my own journey at my own pace.

Philippians 2:13
Philippians 2:16
Ecclesiastes 4:4

The world will exist without me. I am apart of a ripple effect and must leave a lightly lasting impression.

1 John 3:22
Proverbs 25:27
Proverbs 13:22
2 Timothy 3:17

I live an abundant life.

Matthew 6:19-21
Deuteronomy 33:26-27
2 Corinthians 9:8

Candles of Abundant Light

I want everyone in my life and in my presence of this world to live abundantly.

2 Thessalonians 2:16-17
Galatians 6:2
Luke 6:45

Let's Live in the Light

There is more than enough overflow of prosperity and abundance in this world for everyone including me. I must seek it.

Psalms 37:4
Proverbs 16:3
Matthew 5:45

Anything meant for me will be mine in this life.

Romans 11:29
2 Corinthians 9:15
1 Peter 4:10
1 Corinthians 12:4

Let's Live in the Light

I must question my beliefs because they set the foundations for my life. When I change my mind about some things, I also change my life.

2 Thessalonians 2:7-12
John 20:30
Deuteronomy 31:8
Romans 8:6

I choose to do what makes my heart set on fire or I accept I am perfectly content that I am all that I desire to be and contribute to the world existence in time.

2 Timothy 1:6
Ecclesiastes 6:1-9
Philippians 4:11–13
Matthew 24:13
Timothy 6:6-10

Let's Live in the Light

I must know & live my purpose, use my gifts, share my talents, serve, and give in any capacity that I am capable.

Ephesians 3:19-21
Romans 12:6-8
1 Corinthians 12:4-11 & 31
1 Peter 4:10-11

Candles of Abundant Light

I have gifts or talents unique to me.

James 1:17
Ephesians 2:10
1 Peter 4:10
1 Corinthians 12:4–11
Philippians 2:3

Let's Live in the Light

Everyday, I must operate from a sincere authentic place from within me.

Proverbs 27:19
Romans 13:12-13
1 Timothy one:5
1 Peter 1:22

I must believe in myself and keep myself motivated. It is ultimately my own personal responsibility.

John 15:5
Proverbs 3:26
Proverbs 3:5-6
Philippians 4:13

Let's Live in the Light

I must be a better version of me for me
every day.

Philippians 4:13
1 Peter 2:1 -3
1 Corinthians 13:11
Philippians 1:6

I am not smaller or bigger compared to other human beings on this earth.

Psalms 37:23-24
James 1:7
Deuteronomy 8:2
2 Corinthians 10:12
Romans 12:6

I must never compare my life to anyone else's.

Romans 2:11
Galatians 5:24-26
Galatians 6:4
Ecclesiastes 3:18-22

My constant thoughts will make or break me. I must praise myself on both big and small accomplishments equally.

Psalms 131:1-2
Isaiah 40:28-31
Peter 2:9-11

Let's Live in the Light

I must never be my own worst enemy. I must monitor my self-talk to prevent self-destruction.

1 John 5:4
Isaiah 44:22
Hebrew 10:19-23

I have boundaries. I know what is and what is **not** my responsibility in this world.

Romans 12:18-21
1 Corinthians 13:12
Isaiah 40:28–31
Colossians 1:29

Let's Live in the Light

I must identify and implement things into my life that bring me joy and promote self-care.

Ecclesiastes 5:13-20
1 Corinthians 12:4-11
1 Corinthians 10:13

I must only surround myself with those who see the best in me even when I can't, for they will keep me uplifted.

John 15:1-11
Proverbs 17:17
John 15:13
Matthews 15:13-14

The more I mentally repeat a specific thing, the more I continue to relive it emotionally. I release it and easily I will find closure to unnecessary thoughts.

Lamentations 3:26-33
Nehemiah 8:10
2 Corinthians 4:8 -9

I must let go of hurtful thoughts, events that have happened to me in the past, or painful words that have been used against me. Such things will hold me captive to a sunken mental prison where days can turn into dreadful years of hidden sorrow that weighs down my life.

James 1:19
Psalms 19:14
Proverbs 12:18
Proverbs 18:21
2 Timothy 1:7

I must let go and save myself from mental despair. No one can put me in a bad mental space but ME, if I allow myself.

Romans 12:14
Psalms 34:18
John 16:33
Proverbs 17:27

Mindfulness is everything, MY LIFELINE. I must check myself frequently. This dictates who I know I am, the life I will live, and the relationships I have with others.

Romans 12:3-8
Romans 8:12-13
James 3:13-18
Proverbs 17:9

Let's Live in the Light

Align my unconscious and
conscious mind for proper flow
in life. I must do my lifework.

Romans 12:2
1 Peter 4:7
James 1:22
Isaiah 26:3

I must be confident in my
awareness of light provided in
all good or bad situations and
learn from every encounter
while pursuing to move onward.

Philippians 1:6
Proverbs 3:26
Joshua 1:9
Hebrew 13:6
Isaiah 41:10

My story line will change on certain areas in my life based on daily shifts in the way I feel and reason with myself at times.

Philippians 1:6
1 Thessalonians 5:16-18
Hebrews 13:8
Ecclesiastes 1:1-18

Familiar or comfortable things do not mean they are good for me, just as new or unfamiliar things do not mean they may be bad for me.

1 John 4:1
1 John 2:27
1 Samuel 16:7
1 Thessalonians 5:21
Colossians 2:8

Change is everlasting on Earth
and I must evolve continuously;
this will not always be
comfortable.

Hebrew 4:12
1 Corinthians 14:33
1 Timothy 4:1
Hosea 14:9
Proverbs 27:6

I must grow, adapt, and evolve with time as it changes. This is my own responsibility. It is vital for my survival.

Galatians 6:5
Romans 15:13
1 Corinthians 10:13

Let's Live in the Light

I am open to necessary diverse ideas, knowledge, and newest ways to evolve, survive, and succeed in life.

1 Corinthians 13:11-12
Romans 8:28
1 Thessalonians 5:21

I may never get closure on
something that is very
devastating to my life, but my
life must MOVE ON.

Hebrews 10:36-37
Proverbs 20:22
1Thessalonians 5:15

Let's Live in the Light

There are things that will
happen to me in the world that
will cause horrible feelings of
pain, resentment, and moments
that cause me to get lost. I may
feel sunken in darkness
miserably lifeless, but in these
moments I must seek harder to
see and connect to the LIGHT.

Romans 8:11
Philippians 2:12
Matthew 13:43

An owed apology from someone else will not be the master of my life.

Matthew 18:21-22
Proverbs 25:19
Lamentations 3:30-31
Psalms 64:1-10

Let's Live in the Light

My life is my own to value and protect. I must love me protectively every second of each day and value me enough to define healthy boundaries which protect myself.

Ephesians 2:10
Romans 8:31
Genesis 1:26–28
Psalms 139:13
Galatians 1:15

Candles of Abundant Light

I must push forward in life
through both good and bad
times with equal energy.

1 Corinthians 12:6
Philippians 2:13
Isaiah 40:29
1 Peter 4:11
Psalms 19:6

My journey through pain will make me feel devastated, lost, alone, anxious, confused, unloved, without any control, helpless, or lifeless.

Jeremiah 29:11
Proverbs 4:23
Luke 21:14-19
Nehemiah 8:10

Pain is natural for all humans at any one random point in their lives. This is where my greatest strength is demanded of myself.

Psalms 27:13-14
John 16:33
Hebrews 13:5

Let's Live in the Light

I must use my internal and
external support systems in my
life; remembering self-love and
faith are vital.

Proverbs 27:17
Psalms 46:10
Hebrews 11:1
Luke 1:37
Philippians 4:9

I have the power to change my
circumstances.

Proverbs 15:22
James 1:2-4
John 8:12
Proverbs 19:21

I am not a victim in this world.

1 John 5:4
1 Corinthians 10:13
Ephesians 6:13
James 1:1-5
Ephesians 6:10

I must do what is right under all
circumstances.

Luke 6:35
Galatians 5:16-17
Psalms 119:105

I control how busy my life is.

1 John 2:17
Ecclesiastes 3:1-22
Zechariah 4:6
Matthew 6:34
Matthew 11:28

I must continuously create plans and have a purpose. If my plans fail, it only requires a new plan to be created; failure does not mean the end of the world, but a signal to try a new approach.

Proverbs 16:3
Luke 14:28
Proverbs 19:21
Psalms 20:4
Proverbs 16:9

I am in this world but not of this world.

Ecclesiastes 1:1-11
Galatians 5:14-16
John 9:5

I must right my wrongs
whenever possible.

Proverbs 2:13
Proverbs 10:10
Timothy 1:7
Proverbs 10:10

I care enough to help others
find their way through things
authentically and genuinely,
requiring nothing in return.

Romans 12:13
1 Corinthians 15:58
2 Corinthians 1:3–4

I am not defined by my
limitations, mistakes, or
setbacks.

Proverbs 20:27
Proverbs 10:9
Isaiah 43:18
Psalms 51:10

Let's Live in the Light

Not one human on earth is
perfect or without error.

Romans 3:23
Proverbs 14:22
Matthew 22:29
James 5:20
Proverbs 30:5

My trials and errors have taught me priceless lessons, which I can use as testimony to help others.

John 9:25
1 Timothy 6:12
Ephesians 4:15
Luke 6:37
Psalms 119:105

My truths are my everything,
my integrity.

John 14:16
Proverbs 12:22
2 Corinthians 8:21
Titus 2:7

The truth will set me free.
I shall embrace it and allow it
to live within me accepted by
myself and without any
condemnation from myself or
anyone else.

Romans 8:1
Hebrews 13:18
Romans 1:17

There is great power in all truths.

Proverbs 15:11
Psalms 103:12-14
Psalms 119:18

I must welcome truth and
embrace its existence.

Proverbs 24:23
Matthew 5:33-37
1 John 3:18
Ephesians 6:1

Let's Live in the Light

I am entitled to have honor in
my milestones and
accomplishments in life.

Psalms 41:11-12
Colossians 3:23
Philippians 4:8

I must maintain truth with others freely and sustain solidified relationships around me.

John 15:12-13
Proverbs 17:17
Exodus 20:16
Isaiah 26:7

Somewhere in the world,
someone has it worse than me.
I must remain thankful for many
things daily in my life.

Romans 12:12
Hebrews 12:1-2
1 Thessalonians 5:16-18
2 Corinthians 4:15
Colossians 3:15

I must find reasons to be thankful and grateful in everyday with account to all measurements of small to phenomenal. This is a higher critical power source of my light.

Luke 11:34-36
1 Thessalonians 5:16-22
Matthew 13:31-32
Jeremiah 33:3

Let's Live in the Light

I will assist others in seeing
their own reasons to be
thankful and grateful in this
world, so that we may shine
even brighter together.

Romans 12:15
1 Corinthians 2:9-16
Matthew 15:11
Daniel 12:3

I am a unique being living in the light of this world. I am not a color, gender, culture, race, ethnicity, age, skillset, or knowledge level etc.

Hebrew 12:14-15
Romans 12:16
Galatians 3:28
1 Peter 2:9

Let's Live in the Light

Everyone around me enjoys my
presence and I actively seek
ways to enjoy others positively.

Psalms 34:10
Romans 15:13
Psalms 46: 1-3
Isiah 26: 3-4

I am patient as some may need more time to trust, love, understand, respect, or see value in me as I would like. A person or group may never see value in me and this is okay.

Psalms 139:14
Romans 15:7
John 13:34
Leviticus 19:33-34

I will maintain healthy
boundaries.

Galatians 6:5
Proverbs 19:19
2 Thessalonians 3:10
1 John 4:1

Some people have a very valid reason why they are upset or have chosen not to like me. I shall inquire when necessary.

Luke 12:11-12
Romans 12:17-18
Philippians 2:3
Titus 2:7
Proverbs 21:21

Let's Live in the Light

I respect and support others'
choices or space.

Matthew 7:12
Romans 12:10
Philippians 2:3
1 Peter 2:17
1 Corinthians 10:33

I see people as they are,
and **not** as whom I want them
to be.

Proverbs 27:9
Mark 12:29-31
Genesis 3:5
Ephesians 1:18
Matthew 20:33

Let's Live in the Light

I respect others' people's lives
and what they choose to do
with their time.

Acts 5:38-39
John 15:13
Matthew 23:24
Philippians 2:1-30
Isaiah 5:20–21

I am supportive of others. I may not like a specific thing, but it means the world to someone I care about, so I can make sacrifices.

John 13:34-35
1 Thessalonians 5:12-13
Romans 12:10
Philippians 2:3-4

I am aware my actions can be sacrificing to build or sabotaging to destroy my relationships.

Romans 13:7
Luke 6:30-36
Matthew 7:12
James 1:12

Like a glass that is considered either half full or half empty, you can only be moving in one direction toward or away from something or someone in your life. I must be mindful of my own movements and understand motives.

1 Corinthians 10:31
Colossians 3:7
Matthew 5:8
James 4:3
Proverbs 16:2

Let's Live in the Light

I do my best to foster healthy
respectful and loving
relationships in my life, it is
always a dual responsibility.

James 3:17
1 Peter 4:8
Ephesians 4:1-3
Proverbs 18:24

My family and friends require
quality time.

Proverbs 15:17
1 Timothy 5:8
Ephesians 6:4
Joshua 24:15

Let's Live in the Light

People I care about deserve my
undivided attention.

Colossians 3:14
1 Peter 4:1
Romans 12:9-10

One bad day, mistake, or horrible event does not define my whole life; this too shall pass in due time.

Romans 8:38-39
Isaiah 40:29
Psalms 18:16

A person may attempt to fix their mistakes and pain they have caused me at some point in their lives unexpectedly, this is welcomed.

Matthew 4:17
Romans 3:23
Matthew 5:38-42
Luke 17:4
Proverbs 28:13

Problems can be solved, they require me to think clearly and find a solution. Multiple solutions may be required to resolve one problem. This may also require me to seek help from others as I need it.

Proverbs 20:18
Psalms 147:3
John 14:6
Luke 15:7

I must use my energy wisely
and cautiously for my well
being.

Philippians 2:13-16
Matthew 11:28-29
Psalms 68:35
Colossians 1:29

The energy I use to impact
others will be exerted back unto
me as well.

James 1:2-3
Colossians 1:11
Jeremiah 31:25

I must know exactly where my
energy is being depleted. I
must ask is this necessary for a
short term or long term benefit?

Psalms 73:26
Galatians 6:9
Psalms 119:114

I do not focus myself on tiny
things that distract me from the
bigger journey for my life

Psalms 18:31-32
Philemon 1:20
Philippians 3:15-17

Let's Live in the Light

I feel comfortable saying "no"
as equally as I feel very
comfortable saying "yes."

Proverbs 15:16
Matthew 5:6
Psalms 1:1-3
2 Corinthians 1:3-4

I take full responsibility for
events I am allowing to happen
in my life.

Proverbs 15:14
2 Corinthians 4:8-9
James 1:22-24

Let's Live in the Light

I must identify what I need to learn from every experience of my life.

Joshua 1:19
Psalms 119:59-60
Lamentations 3:40

I can face myself and ask real questions such as, "how am I accountable for what is happening and what is my role in this specific thing happening to me right now" *or* "how did I allow this to happen and progress this far?"

2 Corinthians 13:5
Galatians 5:22-23
Romans 12:2

Let's Live in the Light

I will win and lose at unequal
ratios in my life and this is okay.
I must continue to live with
integrity.

Matthew 5:4
Psalms 91:11-12
Proverbs 2:7-9
Psalms 71:20

Pressure is apart of life. I will not react with emotions to see clear through to the answers or desired outcomes.

2 Corinthians 4:16-18
Proverbs 25:28
Matthew 11:28-30
Psalms 55:22
Isaiah 41:10

I appreciate growth
opportunities.

1 John 5:14-15
Proverbs 16:3
Psalms 84:11
Hebrews 11:6

I accept what I can change
when I am ready.

Exodus 18:23
Hebrews 13:8
Deuteronomy 31:8
Psalms 32:8
2 Peter 3:9

Let's Live in the Light

I release regret and solidify in
the acceptance of what I cannot
change for the ultimate survival
of my journey in life. I must
keep moving forward.

Mark 12:30
Job 31:23
Psalms 72:5
Joshua 1:9
Philippians 3:13

I am **never** a victim.

Lamentations 3:37
Psalms 27:4
Hebrews 12:7
James 1:12

I understand that life is not just
about me or evolves only
around me. I am a part of a
beautiful and intertwined ripple
effect of this world.

Ephesians 4:1-5
Matthew 5:5
Philippians 2:4
Luke 6:35

I must seek mentors,
knowledge, networks, trainings,
new environments, support
systems, and all the resources I
can to achieve my goals in
good proper standards or
quality.

Proverbs 15:22
1 Corinthians 3:5-16
Proverbs 3:5-6

Let's Live in the Light

When I learn, achieve, survive,
or master certain things in life,
I must also teach and share it
with others.

Proverbs 15:2
Mathew 5:7
2 Timothy 2:2
James 5:19–20

Iron does sharpen iron and this will not always feel good; this is okay.

Proverbs 27:5
Proverbs 27:17
Philippians 3:17

Unconditional love has no
conditions required of others.

John 15:12
1 John 4:8
1 Corinthians 13:4–7

I must be slow to anger.

James 1:19-20
Proverbs 17:17
Proverbs 29:11

Let's Live in the Light

I must treat my own self with
love and respect at all times.

Proverbs 19:8
Song of Solomon 4:7
Genesis 1:27
Romans 12:2

I provide peace, love, and
respect to anyone in my
presence.

Matthew 10:16
John 7:24
Matthew 5:9
Colossians 3:13
Jude 1:2

Let's Live in the Light

I am not selective in my respect
and humbleness towards
others. I engage with
peacefulness and respect in all
my interactions in this world.

Ephesians 4:3
Philippians 4:9
Psalms 119:165

I will be a servant to a greater cause I know I am ordained to participate in. This is something bigger than just myself to gain fulfillment in life.

1 Corinthians 12:4-11
Matthew 6:1
Matthew 5:16

I commit to selflessness in my
marriage and as a parent.

1 Corinthians 13:13
1 Corinthians 13:4-8
Ecclesiastes 4:9-10
Genesis 2:18
John 13:34

Marriage requires unconditional
love.

Proverbs 31
Colossians 3:19
1 Corinthians 13:13

In marriage when incidents occur I must ask, "Do I want to be right or together?" I must be cautious of the points I want to prove. I must attack problems and not people in my life.

Ephesians 4:2-3
Peter 4:8
Genesis 2:18

There is no proper place for
ego and pride in love.

1 Peter 4:8
Ephesians 5:25
1 John 4:16-18

Parenting is one of the hardest
and most fulfilling life
assignments in this world. I
must take parenting **one** day at
a time.

Proverbs 22:6
Psalms 127:3
1 Corinthians 16:14
Luke 1:37
Deuteronomy 6:6-7

Parenting requires resilience.

Ephesians 4:29
Matthew 6:34
Philippians 4:6
Psalms 127:3

In marriage it requires me to love unconditionally from a selfless space of daily-renewed limitless light found within. There can be no conditions exchanged for sustainability.

1 John 4:8
Romans 13:8
Romans 12:9-10
Genesis 2:24

Nothing can become my idol,
for that gives it massive power
over my life casting blockage of
the light.

Luke 16:13
Exodus 20:5-6
Joshua 1:8
2 Chronicles 16:19
Ecclesiastes 2:1-17

Let's Live in the Light

What would love do in every situation of life? I must live accordingly letting life fall into its divine order.

1 John 4:16-18
Colossians 3:14
1 Peter 4:8

I must forgive in order to
survive in spiritual light and
psychologically to be healthy in
this world. This will require time
and strength of me to focus on
core roots of incidents.

Matthew 6:14
Luke 17:3-4
Hebrew 12:15

I must forgive myself.

Acts 10:15
Ephesians 2:8
Jeremiah 31:3
Romans 3:23

Do not allow resentment to
seed and root itself into your life
today; as it will present itself in
a future day in one way or
another.

Isaiah 40:8
Psalms 32
1 Peter 5:10
Ephesians 4:31

I grant mercy to others to save myself.

Hebrews 4:16
Ephesians 2:4-5
Psalms 51:1-2
Micah 7:18

I may not always understand
the motives or reasons behind
others' choices.

Romans 14:1-2
Psalms 112:5
Isaiah 55:7

Let's Live in the Light

Self-preservation, self-care,
and self-love is a daily priority.

Psalms 34:18
1 Corinthians 6:19–20
3 John 1:2

My health is everything. I must commit to sustain my quality of life for myself and for those who love me. I must listen to my body for it speaks volumes to me.

Proverbs 25:16
1Corinthians 12:14-26
1 Corinthians 10:31
1 Corinthians 6:19–20
3 John 3:12

Let's Live in the Light

Self-care is a vital mandatory
part of each day so that my
light may never subdue to
dimming. It is my responsibility
to protect my inner light.

Proverbs 15:13
Philippians 3:7-9
3 John 1:2
Mark 6:31

I will find thankfulness in every
day.

Jeremiah 15:16
Lamentations 3:22-23
Colossians 2-7
1 Chronicles 16:34

Let's Live in the Light

Everyday, I have tremendous gratitude for the life that has been provided to me to master. I enhance my light contribution during my lifetime and throughout history.

Joshua 1:9
Luke 11:33-36
Ephesians 5:8

Breathing is important.
Remember to breathe, it fuels
clarity into your life.

Isaiah 26:3
Job 33:4
John 20:22
Psalms 150:6

My strength does not come
from food alone.

Psalms 23:1-3
1 Kings 19:4-8
Matthew 5:6
John 6:27
John 4:34

Like a tree balanced firmly planted on both sides, I must balance all or drop something immediately. I must stay balanced allowing nothing to uproot my solidarity.

Proverbs 11:1
Galatians 1:10
Psalms 1:3
Psalms 52:8

Let's Live in the Light

I must grow in influential ways
for others in all areas of my life.

1 Samuel 2:26
Hebrews 6:1
1 Peter 2:2-3
Colossians 1:9-10
Psalms 92:12-14

I must make peace with everyone in my life. This may be self initiated and beneficial for me regardless of the other person's requirement; and this is okay.

Proverbs 20:27
Ephesians 4:2
Matthew 5:9
Romans 14:19
John 14:27

Let's Live in the Light

I must never cast judgment on others for life distributes circumstances randomly and unequivocally to each. No one persons life lived mimics exactly that of another in the existence of time. I must look for the good in all others way of life where possible.

Proverbs 20:23
Proverbs 21:2
Philippians 4:8
Matthew 7:1–5

People change constantly at various rates of swift or slowness; this is a natural part of life.

John 15:1-11
2 Corinthians 4:16-18
2 Corinthians 5:17
Ezekiel 36:26

Let's Live in the Light

I know my limits and I have
boundaries in place that others,
including myself, must respect.

Psalms 103:5
Proverbs 4:23
Romans 12:2
Deuteronomy 19:4

I deserve, need love, and require love. I must be honest with myself, I want to be loved. I want and deserve love more than I fear it.

2 Corinthians 5:7
1 John 4:18
John 13:34–35
1 Corinthians 16:14

My life will never remain the
same over time, this is
impossible.

James 29:11
2 Peter 3:9
Ecclesiastes 3:1
Isaiah 43:19

My life will have many different seasons of changes. Each season will reveal who I am to myself and others. These shifts in the paradigm will rotate people closer or farther away from me during these seasons; and this is okay.

Ecclesiastes 3:1-8
Proverbs 17:17
Proverbs 3:5–6

Sometimes I have priorities and sometimes I don't, and that's okay if I am not defaulting on my responsibilities.

Galatians 6:4-5
Romans 14:10
Peter 1:10
Colossians 3:23-24

I know when to "peace be still"
or "go with the flow" as needed.

John 14:27
Isaiah 26:3
Colossians 3:15
Matthew 5:9

Words have power.

Proverbs 10:11
Proverbs 15:4
Proverbs 23:16

Unspoken words can never be
repeated. Speak from a place
of love at all cost.

Exodus 23:1-3
Philippians 2:14-15
Lamentations 3:26
Psalms 62:5

I understand that different
forms of communication
changes the messages in the
world around me.

Luke 11:28
1 Titus 2:11-12
Proverbs 15:23
1 John 2:15
Mark 8:36

Some questions have a simple "yes" or "no" answer; requiring no additional elaboration.

Colossians 4:6
Psalms 141:3
Psalms 21:23
Psalms 18:2

My words are fruitful and powerful. I will be fruitful in my speaking and expect it in return. If I curse, then I deserve to be cursed.

Proverbs 4:24
Proverbs 25:18
Proverbs 15:28

Words can build or slay
another. Words can change my
own or another's life
permanently forever once
spoken.

Proverbs 15:4
Proverbs 16:24
Proverbs 18:4

Let's Live in the Light

For every negative I think or
speak to someone, I will also
ensure I say a positive.

Proverbs 15:1
Ephesians 4:29
Proverbs 29:11
James 1:19-20

I give praise and compliment to others when it is due. I enjoy empowering others and I enjoy receiving it.

Proverbs 12:25
Proverbs 15:23
Proverbs 15:17
Proverbs 14:25

Let's Live in the Light

I never use my words to break
or hurt another fellow human;
and will never be responsible
for unnecessary pain.

Proverbs 18:20
Proverbs 11:9
Proverbs 11:12
Proverbs 11:17
Proverbs 25:18

I speak up for those who
cannot speak for themselves.

Proverbs 31:8-9
Proverbs 20:15
Proverbs 11:25
Proverbs 3:27-28
Proverbs 14:21

I am silent when I have nothing
fruitful to say. I understand
there is a time to remain silent.

Ecclesiastes 9:17
Psalms 62:5
Psalms 131:2
Ecclesiastes 3:7-8
Proverbs 17:28

Unforeseen gaps happen in
communication.

Proverbs 10:12
Colossians 4:6
Proverbs 18:13
Proverbs 13:17

I will always ask myself, "Is this point I want to prove necessary to make or will it chisel away at a relationship in my life unnecessarily to be forever changed?"

Proverbs 17:28
Proverbs 10:19
Proverbs 231:23

That which I speak of others, I
must hold myself accountable
to the same accord.

Matthew 12:36
Psalms 19:14
James 3:1

I must identify positive words of
affirmation coded specifically
for me to resonate my light in
the darkest of hours.

Ephesians 6:18-19
Jeremiah 15:16
Luke 24:32

Candles of Abundant Light

I will not let insecurities from
within dim my light in any
moment while in this world.

Galatians 5:22
Romans 12:9
Psalms 56:3

The more I repeatedly speak a specific thing or retell an event the more I will continue to relive it.

Proverbs 15:30
Proverbs 15:1
Proverbs 16:24
2 Corinthians 10:5
Romans 8:6

I admit when I am wrong, wow-
how it changes everything in
the situation and maintain the
respect.

Proverbs 3:5-6
Romans 12:12
James 1:2
James 4:17

I must never speak the word
"hate" in any sentence.

James 3:2-12
Proverbs 10:18
Job 5:14
Luke 6:27
Proverbs 10:12

One angle does not provide all the views. I must be open to look through the lens view of others who stood in a different place other than me to gain expanded sight.

John 9:35-41
Acts 17:16-34
Galatians 6:4-5
Proverbs 20:5

I must be an active listener in life.

Proverbs 15:32
James 1:19
Proverbs 18:13 & 15
Proverbs 10:17

Criticism is crucial for my existence.

Proverbs 4:1-9
Job 5:7
Proverbs 15:31
Proverbs 29:23
Proverbs 29:1

I must seek feedback in discussions from those around me to understand how my presence impacts their life. I cannot always rely on my own perception or expectations. It is my decision to use this feedback, which is a perception of me that I may not be aware of. This will help me see how I appear to others from the outside looking in.

Proverbs 25:12
Proverbs 27:6
Proverbs 12:15
James 1:2-3

I will reject and protect from
what is intended to harm me
and receive what is evident.

Proverbs 4:23
Peter 5:8
Ephesians 6:11
Psalms 32:7
Isaiah 54:17

Let's Live in the Light

There are seasons of my life that will be dark and I must fail forward into the next chapter of my life. Failure is not my captain.

2 Peter 1:3-4
Psalm 3:5
Isaiah 43:2

I must seek a mentor in this world and have a support system.

Proverbs 29:26
Proverbs 10:14
Ecclesiastes 7:5

I have options of autobiographies or biopics etc. to discover what happened in this world to others. I can learn from them in many ways such as what motivated them, wisdom provided, or what obstacles crafted who they became.

Proverbs 119:24
Luke 6:43-45
Psalms 119:8

I seek help when I need it. I cannot do everything on my own. I will not always know everything or the best way. There may always be a better way and someone who is willing to help me, this is okay.

Proverbs 3:5-6
2 Corinthians 5:7
Psalms 119:24

Let's Live in the Light

Support and interest groups are
very uniquely resourceful to
your life needs.

Proverbs 27:9
1 Peter 3:9
Hebrews 10:24-25
Deuteronomy 33:27

At work I must commit myself and stay focused on the vision and goals. I must work hard with discipline, commitment, honesty, consistency, and diligently to reap a continued reward.

1 Peter 2:18-25
Proverbs 10:26
Proverbs 28:18
Proverbs 28:19-22
Proverbs 18:9

Let's Live in the Light

Do things right the first time
around in quality, eliminate the
do over effect.

Matthew 7:24-25
Colossians 3:23
Romans 12:2
James 2:18
1 Corinthians 10:31

Candles of Abundant Light

Like stars that never dim their light, I must position myself in the right spaces where my light is seen and shines in the world.

Philippians 4:13
Romans 8:28
Matthew 5:14–16
Exodus 14:14

Let's Live in the Light

I must take nothing personal, all actions define the potential offender and not me.

1 Thessalonians 5:15-16
1 Corinthians 16:13
John 14:27

I decide how I want to feel
about each individual person.

Ephesians 4:32
Malachi 3:18
Psalms 119:125
Romans 12:2
James 1:20

Let's Live in the Light

I must never over consume
myself with unhealthy emotions
which can create a blur.

Proverbs 4:23
Proverbs 14:29
John 14:27
Galatians 5:16–24
Luke 12: 25-26

Candles of Abundant Light

In my family, I will contribute to
their love, strength, and well
being in this world.

Proverbs 27:24
Proverbs 20:20
Exodus 20:12
1 Timothy 5:8
Proverbs 13:22

I treat everyone the way I want
to be treated.

Proverbs 29:5
Matthew 5:43-48
James 2:8-9
Hebrews 12:14

I block no one's blessings and provide as much guidance, support, opportunities, and extend kindness to others as I can.

Proverbs 21:26
Matthew 19:16-22
1 Corinthians 12:7

I balance my giving with my taking. My taking must never exceed my giving. Different ways of giving are monetary, gifting, tithing, caring for, time shared, serving, or teaching others etc.

Romans 12:6-8
Mark 10:21
Proverbs 29:27
1Corinthians 12:4-11
1 Peter 4:9-11

I am thankful for things that
have been given to me in life
and trust in why some things
have also been TAKEN away
by a higher power.

1 John 2:24-25
Job 1:8-12
Psalms 5:8
Psalms 34:19
Proverbs 16:19

I trust and value my own unique journey.

Psalms 91:1-16
Psalms 23:4
Jeremiah 29:11
John 3:16

Time is the ultimate revealer
and healer.

Romans 8:35
Ecclesiastes 3:11
John 6:63
Psalms 31:15
Mark 13:32-33

My territory is limitless as I may
roam into expanded realms
everyday.

Proverbs 25:28
1 John 3:1-13
1 Chronicles 4:10
Proverbs 4:25-27

I must get to know others unfamiliar to me in ethnicity, races, age, languages, business genres, education, experienced backgrounds, professions, careers, university experiences, church locations, religions, politics, travels, neighborhoods, cities, states, regions, etc. to understand how the world works interrelated as one.

Proverbs 13:20
Colossians 3:12-14
Psalms 127:3

Everyone around me in my
immediate circle doesn't have
all the answers I need. I must
seek new & unfamiliar people &
resources to expand my life's
territory.

1 Chronicles 4:10
2 Samuels 22:37
Isaiah 54:2
Deuteronomy 19:8

I am open to inquiring about the
journey of a loved one, friend,
stranger, or foe to learn about
their unique stories. These
stories many times will tend to
"wow" me.

Philippians 2:4
Proverbs 27:9
Psalms 133:1
Romans 12:10-11

Let's Live in the Light

If I wake up looking for positive light and joy I will find it. If I wake up looking for otherwise it will find me.

Philippians 4:8
John 14:27
Matthew 21:22

My neighbors are my friends.

Proverbs 25:21-22
Proverbs 27:10
Matthew 19:18-19
James 2:8
Romans 13:10

Let's Live in the Light

There will be many events of proven resilience in my life to bear witness to. I stand ready to conquer and survive each one in every day.

Psalms 118:24
Romans 8:37
1 John 4:4
Psalms 3:3
Hebrews 12:1

Candles of Abundant Light

My actions define and speak
volumes to the world of me
requiring no inquiry.

Ecclesiastes 12:14
John 16:33
Luke 12:35
Isaiah 55:11
Colossians 3:17

Let's Live in the Light

Whatever evil in my bloodline
cannot manifest through me in
my life line.

Ruth 3:1-18
Luke 3:45-52
Romans 12:19

My reputation will speak for
itself and I do not worry about it
as I give each new day the
absolute best that I am.

Hebrews 11:1-3
Hebrews 12:1-13
Proverbs 10:7

Let's Live in the Light

I have courage to speak up for
matters that lead to the
detriment of myself.

Philippians 4:7
Ephesians 5:11
Proverbs 31:9

Tomorrow will take care of itself, I must live one day at a time. I must be present mentally with no racing thoughts in the "now" to live my moments and capture the full experience in each.

Proverbs 27:1
James 4:13-17
Lamentations 3:22-23

Let's Live in the Light

I seek the good in each day, as
I know that at times darkness
will find me.

John 20:19
Colossians 1:19-20
Psalms 37:5

I must remain authentic at all times.

John 8:22
Philippians 1:6
2 Timothy 2:15
John 17:26

Let's Live in the Light

I must take the mask off, my
private life must align with my
public life.

1 Samuel 16:7
Proverbs 3:1 -4
1 Peter 3:8
1 Timothy 4:4

I understand in life no one owes
me anything.

Mark 12:30
Ephesians 1:2-14
Romans 13:8
Matthew 5:42

Let's Live in the Light

I know that time is promised to
no one on earth.

Mark 13:32-33
Ecclesiastes 1:1-11
Romans 13:11-13
Titus 1:2

Let go of what was and accept
what is.

Isaiah 43:18
John 8:22
Ecclesiastes 3:6
Romans 15:7
1 Peter 5:7–9

Do not underestimate
situations.

Psalms 57:1
Proverbs 25:1-10
Ecclesiastes 3:1- 8

Life will hit me with unexpected powerful blows that will make me feel unconsciously broken apart into lost pieces; lost. Pick up the pieces slowly as things fall apart and come back together eventually for the ultimate good of my life.

Matthew 6:34
Matthew 7:24–25
Proverbs 14:12
Colossians 3:2

I must protect my peace at all
cost.

Hebrews 12:14
Colossians 3:15
1 Peter 5:7
James 3:18
Philippians 4:6

I am a living legacy. I was divinely appointed my life here on earth.

John 15:16
1 Timothy 6:6
Psalms 145:4

I am shalom.

John 14:27
Psalms 85:8
1 Corinthians 1:49
Matthew 5:9
Micah 4:3

I must know my prayer
capability, as well as my human
responsibilities.

Galatians 6:4-5
Philippians 4:6-7
James 5:6
Luke 18:1
Matthew 21:22

Let's Live in the Light

Let there be light on earth as it
is in heaven. I desire daily to be
a part of the light.

Matthew 5:8
Genesis 1:3-4
1 Thessalonians 5:23-26

Daily Practice

Let's Live in the Light

Daily Practice:
1. Wake up, pray, meditate, reflect on my day.
2. Go live a purposeful life and practice my gifts.
3. Be love, receive love, & spread love to others.
4. Be slow to anger or fear.
5. Don't get involved in hate or block anyone else's blessings.
6. Be fruitful in my presence and speaking with all.
7. Do my best.
8. Do what is right.
9. Be thankful for many reasons.
10. Believe in myself.
11. Take care of myself.
12. Take care of my health.
13. Take care of my family.
14. End my day by prayer, meditation, reflect on my day, and then go back to sleep.

Repeat

Daily Practice:
Galatians 6:9-10
Matthew 5:10
1 Corinthians 13:4-7
Ephesians 4:26-27
Proverbs 4:17
Psalm 37:27-28
Proverbs 21:3

About the Author

Dr. Crystal Davison is a native to
Houston, Texas where she currently
resides.
She professionally practices as a
pharmacist with a Doctoral degree in
Pharmacology from Texas Southern
University College of Pharmacy and
Health Sciences.

Crystal writes books of poetry,
spirituality, and self help/transformation
which she believes is her true gift and
passion in life.

Candles of Abundant Light

These forms of her writing portray
natural insight on day to day life of
human thoughts and emotions, which is
so graciously depicted connecting to her
readers. Crystal has 4 additional
published works for her readers.

Crystal only desires that her
poetry, writings, and self transformation
tools be the light of others familiarity,
pleasure, or even learning experiences
in life which is captured.

Crystal is happily married and is a very
proud mother.

www.CrystalDavison.com

Davison Publishing Co.
Cypress,Texas

232

Let's Live in the Light

Thank you for your time!